D0243557

THIS WALKER BOOK BELONGS TO:

First published 1995 by Walker Books Ltd
87 Vauxhall Walk, London SE11 5HJ

This edition published 1996

2 4 6 8 10 9 7 5 3 1

This book has been typeset in Garamond.

Printed in Hong Kong

British Library Cataloguing in Publication Data
A catalogue record for this book is available
from the British Library.

ISBN 0-7445-4306-1

CHARLIE AND TYLER AT THE SEASIDE

Written and illustrated by HELEN CRAIG

WALKER BOOKS
AND SUBSIDIARIES
LONDON • BOSTON • SYDNEY

One warm sunny day,
Charlie the country mouse
was sitting on the porch of
his comfortable home in the
hedgerow. He was reading
a letter from his cousin Tyler
the town mouse.
This is what it said:

Dear Charlie,
How's life with you?
As dull as ever, I expect.
Well, now's your chance to
do something exciting. Meet
me tomorrow at the old oak
tree an hour before sunrise
for A DAY AT THE SEASIDE!
love, Tyler

"Oh dear!" said Charlie.
"I don't want to do
something exciting.
I'm quite happy here."
But next morning he
got up while it was still
dark, shouldered his
old satchel and set off
all the same.

Tyler was waiting for him
by the oak tree, rigged out
in a sailor's jersey and a
sea captain's hat.
"Ahoy there!" he called.
"Here comes Mrs Pigeon.
She's going to give us a lift."

The sun was just rising as Mrs Pigeon set Charlie and Tyler down on the seashore.

"Have a lovely day," she said. "And don't forget, meet me on the cliff top at sunset and I'll take you home."

They looked around them. Out of the mist loomed a big shape.

"It's a motorboat!" said Tyler. "Let's go for a trip. I'll be captain because I know about boats. Welcome aboard, Able-seaman Charlie."

Tyler looked around for the controls, but he couldn't find any. "Ah!" he said. "Just a small setback. Let's wait until the mist clears." So the two little mice settled down in the cabin for a snooze.

They were woken by a loud whirring noise. "What's happening?" squeaked Charlie. Waves were flashing past the windows.

"We're at sea – I think," said Tyler as the boat lurched one way and then the other.

"Can't you stop it?" Charlie wailed. "You're captain." But Captain Tyler had no idea *what* to do.

The two mice scrambled on deck and hung on tight. The boat was

speeding madly all by itself, backwards and forwards across the water.

They were frightened for their lives.

At last the boat hurtled towards the shore and hit a rock.
Charlie and Tyler were catapulted into the air and landed – SPLASH! – in a shallow pool.
"Oh dear, oh dear," said Charlie.

But Tyler picked himself up and looked around.

"Let's go beachcombing," he said.
"What's beachcombing?" asked Charlie.
"It's looking for treasure and useful things in the sand," Tyler replied, marching off.

He soon found a little sword that had once belonged to a toy soldier, and a metal badge that made a perfect shield.

Charlie found a parasol and a little bell on a chain. "This will be just right for my front door," he said. He was beginning to enjoy himself. They set off again, their bags laden with treasure.

At last they found themselves under the pier.
"Hey, we can have some fun up there!" said Tyler. "It's only a little climb."
Charlie looked up with a sinking heart. But a great big dog was
lolloping towards them. He had no choice but to follow.

Way down below, the waves
splashed and the dog barked.
"This is scary," said Charlie.
"Nonsense!" said Tyler.

Underneath the floorboards of the pier they found a hole and squeezed through into a very strange place.
"Oh, Tyler!" said Charlie. "What HAVE you got us into now?"

They climbed on and up
into a dimly-lit room
full of shadowy figures.
"Where can we be?"
whispered Charlie.
All of a sudden lights
came on, a curtain
went up and music
began to play. They
were in a toy theatre!

With a whirring of the cogwheels
below, the little figures began to
move in time to the music. Tyler and

Charlie pretended they were part of the show, but too late – they'd been spotted. It was time for a quick exit.

"Phew!" puffed Tyler. "I'm hungry after all that. Let's find some food."

They had sausages, crisps, popcorn and a nice piece of toffee-apple...

And they did very well when it came to ice-cream.

They visited the aquarium
and the hall of mirrors.
All too soon it was time
to go and meet Mrs Pigeon.

Up on the cliff they sat
and watched the boats
out at sea. Charlie liked
it. It was almost as
peaceful as his home
in the hedgerow.

Then a terrible thing happened.
A huge seabird swooped down and grabbed Tyler in its claws.
"Help! Help!" he squeaked. Charlie watched in horror as the great bird carried Tyler far away.

Charlie began to cry. His eyes were so full of tears that he didn't see the bird turn in a circle and head back to her home under the cliff.

The bird dropped Tyler into the nest next to her waiting chick and flew off again. The chick was always hungry and Tyler was to be its next meal.

The chick moved closer to Tyler.

It gave him a peck.

Tyler was furious
and drew his sword.

"Take that!"
he shouted.
"Ow!" squawked
the chick.

The awful noise they made floated up to Charlie, alone and sad on the cliff top. He crept to the edge and peeped over. He couldn't believe his eyes.

"Hang on, Tyler!" he shouted. "I'm coming!" He started off down the cliff without a thought for the dangers below, tumbling, bouncing and sliding until he landed in a small bush just above the nest.

Quickly he pulled the little bell from his satchel
and lowered it down above Tyler's head.
"Grab hold and I'll pull you up," he shouted.

Tyler swung dangerously
over the sea. Charlie pulled
as hard as he could.

The chick squawked, but
by the time the mother bird
came back, Tyler was gone.

Charlie and Tyler scrambled to the top of the cliff where Mrs Pigeon found them later, lying exhausted under some large leaves.
"You poor things!" she cooed. "You do look tired. Climb in the postbag and I'll fly you home."

The two mice took a last look at the seaside. It all seemed so peaceful from the air.
"Charlie, you're a hero," said Tyler. "You saved my life."

It was night when Mrs Pigeon put them down by the hedgerow.
"Goodbye and thanks," they called.

Safe and sound at Charlie's home, they sat on the porch and talked over all that had happened.
"What a fine adventure we had!" said Tyler. Charlie wasn't so sure. However, on one thing they did agree – they had both been terribly, terribly BRAVE!

MORE WALKER PAPERBACKS
For You to Enjoy

THE TOWN MOUSE AND THE COUNTRY MOUSE
retold and illustrated by Helen Craig

Shortlisted for the Smarties Book Prize

"Helen Craig's spirited retelling ... is the best version of this old favourite for many years." *The Economist*

0-7445-3151-9 £4.50

MARY MARY
by Sarah Hayes/Helen Craig

Included on the list of texts to be used in conjunction with the Standard Assessment Tasks of the National Curriculum (Key Stage 2, Level 1 – 2)

"Giants are always popular with children and this fairy tale has a friendly giant and an intrepid heroine, two excellent ingredients for a winning story." *Child Education*

0-7445-2062-2 £4.50

THIS IS THE BEAR
by Sarah Hayes/Helen Craig

Three rollicking rhymes about the adventures of a boy, a dog and a bear.

"For those ready for their first story, there could be no better choice... Helen Craig's pictures are just right." *Judy Taylor, The Independent*

0-7445-0969-6 *This Is the Bear*
0-7445-1304-9 *This Is the Bear and the Picnic Lunch*
0-7445-3147-0 *This Is the Bear and the Scary Night*

£4.50 each

Walker Paperbacks are available from most booksellers, or by post from B.B.C.S., P.O. Box 941, Hull, North Humberside HU1 3YQ
24 hour telephone credit card line 01482 224626

To order, send: Title, author, ISBN number and price for each book ordered, your full name and address, cheque or postal order payable to BBCS for the total amount and allow the following for postage and packing:
UK and BFPO: £1.00 for the first book, and 50p for each additional book to a maximum of £3.50.
Overseas and Eire: £2.00 for the first book, £1.00 for the second and 50p for each additional book.

Prices and availability are subject to change without notice.